Storm 7

HOPE YOU
ENJOY THIS
READ

BEN WALKER

Copyright © 2017 by Ben Walker

All rights reserved.
No part of this publication may be reproduced, distributed, or transmitted in any form or by any means, including photocopying, recording, or other electronic or mechanical methods, without the prior written permission of the publisher, except in the case of brief quotations embodied in critical reviews and certain other non-commercial uses permitted by copyright law.

This book is a work of fiction. Names, characters, place and incidents are either the product of the author's imagination or are used fictitiously/contextually with purpose. Any other resemblance to actual persons, living or dead, business establishments, events or locales is entire coincidental.

The moral right of the author has been asserted

Text copyright © Ben Walker, 2017
All Rights Reserved

Printed in the United States of America

Editor(s) : Ben Walker, Ronald Tremblay, Jak Spencer

STORM 7

Paperback 5" x 8"

Paperback 12.7 x 20.32 cm

www.bjwalker.co.uk

About the Author

Ben Walker is a student who currently finds a hobby in writing novels/short stories. His latest work, Storm 7, is a novel about an elite SWAT team who must face their toughest challenge yet when a casino heist goes horrifically wrong.

Ben was born in England on February 16th, 2002 and grew up in Leeds, yet currently resides in Kirklees.

He has become an Amazon best-seller in both "Fiction" (#68), "Historical Fiction" (#5) and "Teen & Young Adult" (#17) short story categories.

<u>STORM 7</u>

Introduction

This book is inspired by Rainbow Six, a novel by Tom Clancy. I discovered the idea of writing my own self-published books by reading other peoples, and noticing that Amazon had their own free publishing program. I thought I'd try it out by putting a story I wrote in English class online for free. It ended up becoming a best-seller and motivated me to write something bigger, something better. Much bigger. That brought me here, and I was thinking of topics to write about when actually playing the video game adaptation of the novel. Having that as an idea then caused me to remember Rainbow Six Vegas, which I played when I was young on the PSP. Overtime, ideas popped into my head; a casino heist, a big antagonist, and much more. I hope you enjoy this journey I've created, because doing this has been a blast.

Thank you.

Special Thanks

I would like to give special thanks to several people for helping me with the creation of this book. Without these people, most of this would not have been possible.

I'd like to thank my good friend Ronald for helping oversee editing in this book, and for helping me with the cover art, narrative ideas and doing some research.

I'd also like to thank my long-time friend Jak for helping with editing and giving narrative ideas.

I'd love to thank my English teacher for encouraging me to begin writing and entering some short story competitions.

Thanks to RJ for support and help with some audiobooks!

Finally, a special thanks to my family, who wouldn't shut up about this project the entire way through writing it.

Contents

ABOUT THE AUTHOR 4

INTRODUCTION 5

SPECIAL THANKS 6

CONTENTS 7

PROLOGUE 10

CHAPTER 1 13

    PROMOTION 13
    THE TEAM 16
    TRAINING 18
    REMEMBRANCE 23

CHAPTER 2 26

    INVESTIGATION 26
    NARCOTICS 29
    UPSTAIRS 31
    DINING ROOM 33
    MAN DOWN 35
    TRAP DOOR 39

CHAPTER 3 43

    FABIAN JUREWICZ 43
    CRIMSON 45

CHAPTER 4 56

    CONSEQUENCES 56

CHAPTER 5 59

    24 HOURS 59
    THE LEAD 62

BEN WALKER

CHAPTER 6 64
    THE HEIST 64
    CONFESSION 66
    LAST RESORT 69

CHAPTER 7 74
    DIAMOND PLAZA 74
    IDENTITY 82
    LOOSE ENDS 86
    WATER MIXED WITH BLOOD 89

EPILOGUE 97

STORM 7

"Good people sleep peaceably in their beds at night only because rough men stand ready to do violence on their behalf."

- George Oswell

# Prologue

The sound of canisters sliding under the door echoed through their ears.

A few seconds of silence. Dreadfully awaiting the go ahead. He took a deep breath.

"GO GO GO"

Matt turned and lunged at the door with his foot, smashing it down with brute force.

As the door fell, the world slowed down. The sudden explosive noises flew and knocked down Matt; it was too loud. He looked around, seeing his companions rush past him to clear the room. Bright flashes originated from the barrels of their guns as they screamed something incomprehensible. There was a painful ringing in Matt's ears and it was unbearable.

The canisters activated, letting smoke fill the air and block any possibility of vision the enemy might have. The whole squad were wearing their gas masks, and thus were not affected by the impending toxicity of the tear gas. Shot after shot after shot, scream after scream. Until silence.

You could hear heavy breathing through Wayne's mask, he was worn out. They all looked around the room, pointing their barrels at each individual possible hiding spot. Bill kicked the limp arm of a body on the

STORM 7

floor. No movement. Not even a chest inflating and deflating. "We got one down."

"Make that three." mentioned Wesley. "We got two here, I shot one."

Liam nodded at him.

"Room is clear. We have two suspects unconscious and three down." exclaimed Liam into his radio.

"Copy that. I'm seeing two in the corridor." Craig mentioned.

They immediately got to work. Andy went over to Matt and helped him up.

"This is a big one, lads. They know we're here now and they will do anything to get out of here. Be smart and don't rush."

They all lined up against the doorway, signalling each other to get in position through subtle hand gestures. Wayne pulled out his flashbang and held his hand on the pin and trigger.

But before they could breach, they heard the static on Liam's radio increase.

"Hello?" Liam questioned into his radio.

All he heard in response was breathing. Heavy breathing.

BEN WALKER

Someone was listening.

STORM 7

Chapter 1

Promotion

"Sergeant Williams, you are being promoted to Staff Sergeant and as a result you are assigned to command the squad Storm 7, effective immediately." Commander Larson had told him.

"It... Wow. What an honour, sir. Thank you."

Charlie didn't know what to say, if he even had anything *to* say. His own squad? This was a dream come true, and he wasn't going to let anyone down. Charlie had aimed for this his whole career... and now... It was here.

His first task of the day was to introduce himself to the group., so he walked into the office labelled 'Storm 7'.

Charlie noticed that an entire group was sitting in the briefing room talking to each other.

Muttering inundated the whole room, until they spotted him walk through the open door passively.

The sudden silence empowered Charlie.

"Hello, officers. I'm going to be taking control of this squad from now on. My name is Staff Sergeant Williams and I'm very glad to be here. Why don't we... uh... go around and introduce ourselves one after the other?"

Josh started howling with laughter.

"Are you having a laugh? We're not in bloody Alcoholics Anonymous, mate."

Right off the bat; someone who is up to no good. Charlie dealt with his fair share of infantile adults.

"No, but you are in a squad which is going to take itself seriously under all circumstances. Am I clear?"

Josh was leaned back in a metal folding chair with his arms crossed.

"Mate, just beca-"

"Sir."

"Excuse me?"

"You will address me as 'Sir'. Not 'mate'."

"Oh, sorry, you think I want to take orders from you? You're only here mate because the last guy was shot in the fucking chest."

Charlie was shook. Shot? No one told him about that.

"Can you just shut your mouth for one goddamn minute, Josh?" muttered Andy. "Like Jesus Christ, you just never shut up. This guy is the team leader now, grow up and accept it or you'll get us all fired."

"Oh, piss off, Andy. You're the one who got us into this mess."

"ME? You were too busy talking to hear us asking for backup, you moron!"

STORM 7

"I was briefing the General on the situation! Maybe you should have SPOKEN UP."

"ENOUGH", Charlie roared. The whole room went quiet.

"You know what? Fine. I'll play your little game, 'Sergeant Williams'. But if you think, even for a second, that I'm not just here because I have to feed myself, then you have another thing coming."

"Dismissed."

The Team

There were ten men. Josh, Andy, Wesley, Craig, Liam, Bill, Brad, Wayne, Clifford and Matt.

Commander Larson was the Officer in Charge, but didn't get involved in incidents. He usually left it to the team leader, Charlie.

Josh Taylor was the one who never grew up. If he trained as much as he talked, he'd probably be up for SEAL Team Six.

Andy Neilson was a negotiator and a trained medic. He obeyed every order given to him and loved his job, as stressful as it was.

Brad Sullivan carried a ballistic shield and was the first to breach into a room. His only quirk; he couldn't talk. Brad was mute from birth.

Liam Donovan was a risk-taker, and he was the "Point"; usually the first to get into the action.

Wesley Smith and Craig Posner were friends since high school, and stuck together most of the time. Wesley was a sniper; he usually watched through windows for hostiles on roofs or in sight, and Craig was his counterpart; an observer. He usually spotted enemies, and Wesley took them down.

Bill Spade was known as the Armorer; he inspected, maintained and repaired all the weapons on the team.

STORM 7

Wayne Lester was good at tactics; he'd plan out breaching routes and possible offensive strategies. He was a breacher and a perfectionist.

Clifford Robinson was a trainer and a veteran; he'd give advice and training to the rest of the group when the team leader wasn't present.

Matt Jackson was new to the squad; he only recently joined so his job was mainly assisting the others. This didn't mean he was afraid to get his hands dirty.
.

Training

The squad woke up to a twenty minutes' walk-jog, ten tricep dips, five dorsal raises, with only thirty seconds between sets. Some days they would just run for hours. Some they would go swimming, cycling, rowing, or walking for twenty minutes at a time. These were part of their yearly sixteen-week program for fitness and training. On the training side of things, they would have to visit the shooting range for hours at a time and beat each other's scores. Testing various weapons; the M16A2, the M4A4, the M1911, and a Heckler & Koch G3.

Then, onto lethal and non-lethal explosives; an M84 stun grenade, an M67 fragmentation grenade, and a Mk 3A2 concussion grenade. To top it off, they also practiced using pepper spray and handcuffs. Liam loved training; he got a chance to try out all the various weaponry. He was the finest shot in the team; could probably hit a target between the eyes on his first try if he wanted. The fastest time to go through the training range was 32.469 seconds, held by Wayne. The squad then completed hostage training, where they had to shoot a suspect with a human shield. Finally, the squad went for lunch.

STORM 7

"What's your secret, Wayne?" speculated Josh, while filling his mouth with an Extra Value cheeseburger, and chomping down.

"My… secret?" questioned Wayne in response.

"You got the fastest time. Even beat Old Clifford over here."

"Oh… heh… well I always try to predict where the target is going to pop up and pre-fire it."

"We all know that's bullshit."

"Well, what do *you* think my secret is, Josh?"

"That your girlfriend up in that booth is slowing down the timer for you."

"She's not my-"

"Sure, mate."

They all emanated a laugh through their mouths stuffed with food.

"What are you laughing about, lads?"

Charlie walked up to them, holding his tray and smirking.

"Nothing. Just debating on how Wayne got the fastest time yet it takes about 10 minutes just for his brain to power up in the morning." joked Wesley.

They all chuckled, except Josh. Josh was eyeballing Charlie; he didn't belong here. He hadn't been through what they had. He wasn't like them; he was just another leader that will come and go.

"If she's not taken by you, Wayne, then I'm swooping in like a bird of prey." warned Bill.

"Who?" questioned Charlie.

"Lass who runs the shooting range. And the timer with it." replied Liam.

Charlie grinned. "Bit of cheating we got here, eh Wayne?"

"No, sir. Absolutely not."

"Relax. I'm just messing with you."

Another chuckle across the group. As the laughter settled down, Craig had something to point out.

"Huh. Last time we saw you, sir, you were very…"

"Strict? Yeah. Well, it's not a very formal atmosphere, is it? I mean… there's some guy ravaging the bin there for a coin he just dropped." Charlie replied sarcastically.

Even more laughter. Josh tried to hide a grin appearing on his face. They were in a fast food outlet; quite close to the range, few miles out.

They had stopped there when getting fuel for their SWAT van. Imagine that parked outside a gas station.

"Isn't it time we get back?" suggested Josh. Charlie was winning them over, and he didn't like it.

"Speak for yourself, Josh. I've barely eaten my fries." Craig was filling himself. Josh scowled.

STORM 7

"Screw this. I need a whizz." Josh stormed off into the bathroom.

"What's his deal?" asked Charlie.

"Call it a guess; but I just don't think he likes you. Probably wrong though."
Andy's sarcasm never failed to amuse the squad.

Josh slammed shut the cubicle door in anger, sat down, and sighed with his head in his hands. He heard a faint whisper in the cubicle on his right; only a few things were picked up.

"Maestro on 5th", and "cash".

He heard something else… he almost distinguished it but couldn't quite tell what was said. This was before he heard a phone hang up and the man leave in a rush. As any other person would do, he ignored it. He returned to the booth, and noticed everyone packing up and laughing.

What did he say? The thought kept clouding Josh's mind. The man said *something* but it wasn't English. It had the word 'Crimson' at the end and started with… ugh, what was it!? Lunge leave? It would bug him all day.

They were on their way back to the station in the truck. Matt was driving – he knew this van inside and out; had to, he stayed inside for most operations and surveilled the area. It was just before 2pm and they were driving down Route 15 into North Las Vegas.

BEN WALKER

Storm 7 was a division of the Las Vegas Metropolitan Police Department, and were rarely sent out as there were no major crimes in the big city. They didn't have jurisdiction in North Las Vegas, so driving through and spotting criminals angered them all. They were separate from the LVMPD SWAT team, who were a nationally respected organization and composed of up to 40 operators, while Storm 7 had 11. However, even though Storm 7 was a relatively new squad, they were more experienced and highly trained than the LVMPD, dealing with more extreme situations.

After driving past Downtown Las Vegas and exiting the freeway onto South LV Boulevard, they arrived at the station. The squad unloaded from the vehicle, walked inside, pressed 4 on the elevator, and waited. Craig sighed.

"We're one of the best SWAT teams in the state and here we are, locked up in a common police station.".

"That's the way it is, I guess." replied Charlie.

<u>STORM 7</u>

Remembrance

The elevator doors opened, revealing a noisy office. It had your usual police station atmosphere; people muttering, fax machines and printers whirring, coffee pouring, etc. They walked past all the desks full of paperwork and went through a door marked 'Storm 7'. Craig and Wesley went straight into the showers. Liam sat at his desk and leaned back in his chair; closing his eyes for a quick nap.

When you're an elite SWAT team, you rarely get called out unless a big event occurs. Little did they know; the start of the biggest challenge in their careers was about to occur.

"Turn on the TV, will ya'?" groaned Matt.

Wayne reached for the remote and turned on the wall-mounted television. It was mostly used for briefing and presentations, but not in here. The guys liked to watch sports and HBO.

But just by coincidence, the TV was defaulted to the local news channel, Channel 13. Josh was walking past towards the showers as he overheard the television.

"Længe Leve Crimson."

"These are the words most will remember tonight, as yet another casino has been robbed in broad daylight."

BEN WALKER

"This is the third time this year that a Casino has been robbed without any explanation or trace. Staff report that there was no suspicious activity except for one individual in a hoodie, who walked into a staff only doorway and wasn't seen again. Then during the deposit of the profit they made that day, employees noticed the vault was perfectly empty. Not a single dollar bill was left behind."

Josh immediately turned back and walked into the room that the TV was emanating its deafening news from. Matt was slouched in a chair, and noticed Josh walking in.

"Bet you wonder how they pulled that off."

The news report carried on as Josh sat down next to Matt, mesmerized by the TV.

"What casino was this?" Josh questioned Matt without even turning to look at him, his dead expression hypnotised by the news report.

"Why?"

"What… casino… was this…?"

But Josh already knew the answer.

STORM 7

"Maestro Casino."

Chapter 2

Investigation

Josh was stuck at work all night answering questions from a team of investigators who were working the Crimson Case.

"What did this man sound like?" Detective Harris, the lead investigator on the case, asked.

She was wearing a dark grey t-shirt, accompanied by a police belt buckled around midnight black denim jeans. Her arms were crossed yet you could see past her defying stare and notice a pinch of excitement from their first lead.

"He sounded... fairly British." replied Josh, trying to piece together his memories.

"British...?" another detective questioned.

"Yeah."

Harris got closer to Josh. Almost too close.

"You're lying." she cold-heartedly declared.

"You think I'm a liar? Look, I'm a cop like you, why would I lie?"

"Because we know that Crimson is Polish, not British."

"And... you know this how?"

Harris didn't feel the need to explain herself to him, but proceeded anyway. She stated how CCTV footage from a previous casino had

STORM 7

shown the same person, and that was it. Just the single person. He did not contact anyone prior to or after the heist. He was not seen even remotely opening his mouth.

The investigators had used CCTV footage to discover the man's identity. He was Fabian Jurewicz, a Polish immigrant who had recently purchased a house near to the Las Vegas strip.

"But buying land near there would cost a fortune…" Josh pitifully pointed out.

"Yes, but you could easily afford living near to the Las Vegas strip if you robbed three whole casinos."

Some hours later, they had finally finished asking their questions.

"We're done here, thank you for your co-operation, Mr…"

"Carter."

"Mr. Carter. Well, have a safe trip home."

BEN WALKER

Detectives. A weird bunch.

STORM 7

Narcotics

It was the next day, and the squad were gearing up to serve a narcotics search warrant. A package was intercepted at the U.S Customs and Border Protection and an investigation had since led back to some crackheads in Spring Valley.

They had loaded into their truck and driven straight down to the location. Upon reaching the house, they left the vehicle and lined up against the front porch door. Liam gestured to Brad to kick down the door. He nodded, turned, and with a forceful thrust, left the door completely open. Charlie held up three fingers, which slowly became two, and then one finger pointing towards the door violently. All eleven men rushed in. Brad first, Liam second, with the rest following behind.

"Police, put your hands in the air!" boomed Andy as they cleared the room. They pointed their guns all around, looking for movement. That was when a man popped up from behind a table, holding a 9mm handgun.

"Die, pigs!" he screamed as he aimed at the nearest officer; Charlie.

The man readied his fingers around the trigger… and fell to the floor following a shot from Wayne that hit him directly in his abdomen.

BEN WALKER

"One down; Wesley, Liam and Craig take upstairs, Brad, Andy and Bill take the dining room, we'll clear the Kitchen, then rendezvous back here." ordered Charlie.

STORM 7

Upstairs

They all got to work. Wesley, Liam and Craig ran upstairs and lined up outside the bedroom door, packed against the wall. Liam got out his Under-Door Camera and slid it through the airhole under the door. He looked at the screen.

"Two hostiles sat up on the bed." he cautiously whispered.

Through the camera, he could see that one of the suspects was on the phone. She was smoking a cigarette while staring deeply into the wall; focused entirely on the conversation.

"COPS?" she yelled, alarmed.

"Where are you then? Okay, stay there, I'm coming to you."

Then she turned towards the second suspect, a middle-aged man.

"We gotta go, Pete."

She grabbed Pete's arm and started running towards the window.

"We have to breach. Now." mentioned Wesley.

Liam nodded and retracted his camera. He then turned until his back was against the wall, grabbed his MP5, and gave the signal to Craig.

The door flew open with one powerful and calculated shot from Craig's Remington 1100 into the lock.

BEN WALKER

"GET ON THE GROUND, POLICE" Wesley yelled while running into the room, pointing his laser sight at the suspects.

They both stopped dead in their tracks, and slowly raised their hands.

"Shit." the woman muttered under her breath.

STORM 7

Dining Room

Brad, Andy, and Bill all rushed into the dining room. Brad first, with the rest behind the cover of his tall and metal ballistic shield. They split up as they searched the room, looking at every corner and hiding spot. They had no such luck in finding any suspects, and so proceeded to look around cautiously.

Andy noticed that the floor broke away in a certain spot; it was a trap door.

"Guys, you might wanna see this." he turned towards the other two, who were looking in all the cupboards and cabinets for any evidence they could use.

"What'd you find?" Bill curiously queried.

"I think it's a trap door." Andy replied.

"Nice find. Let's not go in there until the rest of the house is clear." Bill recommended.

"Good idea. Let's head back to the dining room and wait for the others."

They walked back; once again holding their guns to every corner in-case a suspect popped out with a weapon.

That's when they heard their radio receive a transmission. As they heard it on the radio, they also heard it in synchronization with a noise originating upstairs. A gunshot.

"WE NEED BACKUP. GET UP HERE." pleaded a voice on the radio.

"What happened!?" interrogated Andy.

"We got a man down."

STORM 7

Man Down

They rushed upstairs, not caring about caution or safety. They cared more about each other.

Each step caused their backpacks to bounce over their shoulders as they sprinted up each individual block of wood on the staircase. Faster and faster, until they reached the top and noticed a door wide open. The door had a bullet hole where the handle would be from a shotgun blast, but it was also smeared in blood.

They screamed their various catchphrases such as "POLICE, GET ON THE GROUND" and "PUT YOUR HANDS WHERE I CAN SEE THEM" as they raided the room.

Upon rushing into the room they noticed quite a few things. One, there was an officer laid against the wall with a silver-engraved kitchen knife dug into his shoulder. Two, there was a woman running for the window. And three, there was a dead body on the ground.

A middle-aged man with a bullet between his eyes, and a handgun laid in his gripless palm.

BEN WALKER

After noticing the new batch of officers, the woman glanced over her shoulder and exclaimed

"I'VE KILLED ONE, I'LL KILL YOU ALL"

before diving out of the window.

Usually one might have run after her, but considering the circumstances of an officer being critically injured, this was not the time.

They turned towards the bleeding cop to notice that it was in-fact Liam, and ran to help.

"Liam!" Andy shouted while kneeling down next to him.

"Jesus Christ!"

He pulled out the knife, and blood started gushing out of the wound. He then immediately took off his gloves and used them to cover it up and apply pressure.

"You're going to be okay, Liam. It's all going to be okay." Andy reassured him of hope.

"What the FUCK happened, guys?" Andy turned towards Wesley and Craig, who had returned from taking cover, and were feeling dreadfully guilty.

"We were going to arrest both of the suspects and… uh… as we were walking towards them they turned and the guy shot at

STORM 7

us so we took cover behind the bed. Because we were taking cover, the woman grabbed a knife off of the drawer and lunged over the bed and stuck it into Liam's shoulder. We popped up and Wesley shot the male suspect before we called for help. You guys got here just in time, I thought that bitch was gonna kill us all." explained Craig.

"Well, she's not going to be killing any of you. We're gonna get Liam some treatment and he's going to be fine." Andy was determined.

Their radios intercepted a signal.

"Is everything okay up there?" emitted Charlie.

"No, sir. Liam's been stabbed in the shoulder." Wesley muttered.

There were a few seconds of silence; the void filled with white noise.

"I see. We're coming up there."

"Wait!" Bill had remembered something and called into his radio to Charlie.

"What is it?" Charlie replied in question.

"The whole house isn't clear yet, we can't let our guard down."

"What room didn't we check?"

Andy knew exactly what Bill was referring to.

"There is a trap door inside the Dining Room floor, sir. We believe some suspects may be down there."

"I see."

The radio was silent for a few seconds. They could tell Charlie was thinking.

After some contemplation, Charlie picked back up his radio.

"Stay there, we have enough men here to go down and clear out that room. Just make sure Donovan is safe, take him out the house."

Charlie knew he shouldn't be talking, they weren't allowed to talk to each other until after the operation was complete, but this was an exception.

STORM 7

Trap Door

Charlie and the remaining four men ran into the dining room with their firearms held high. They were in a caterpillar formation, holding onto one another's shoulder while running in. After double-checking that the room was clear, they all looked around on the floor for a hatch.

They were careful to not make noise as to alert any suspects in the hidden room.

"Over here." whispered Josh.

There was a square flat break-away cover over a hatch in the floor. The only way you could have possibly noticed it is because it was slanted; not fully sealed. This might have been a product of suspects hiding in a rush.

Everyone gathered around the trap door and opted to use hand signals.

They lifted the cover.

BEN WALKER

All they could see was darkness followed by an ominous neon green light. There was a crimson ladder which led down into the seemingly endless abyss.

Wayne threw down a flashbang, and they all looked away. With a boom and a puff of smoke rising out of the hole, groans were heard inside. There *were* suspects down there.

They had to get in there, fast.

Without Brad or Liam to go in first, it was up to Charlie to lead the pack. He put his G36C on his back, mounted the ladder and slid down. The rest of the group followed, one by one sliding down the red ladder.

Charlie landed, turned and immediately opened fire on the silhouette of a suspect with a weapon. Blood smeared onto the wall behind him, which was illuminated by the green projected from the neon light.

He noticed that the room was not just a safe room, but a meth lab. This was great for the detectives back home.

As he heard the others landing behind him, he rushed to cover behind a couch.

Gunshots sent the room into a frenzy, with bullets flying overhead from every angle.

Matt and Wayne took cover next to Charlie, and Matt whispered in his ear.

STORM 7

"There's two more, behind the counter with the beakers on it."

Charlie made a hand signal, nodded to him, peeked out of cover and gave suppressive fire towards the counter as Josh ran to cover behind a fridge.

Matt popped out and shot at the counter with his single-fire G3. It took just three shots to take out the second-to-last suspect; who's head whiplashed from the impact of a bullet to the brain.

"That's another down. One left." Wayne added, before unpinning and throwing his last flashbang over the couch.

As it detonated, a crackle formed in his ear, but he was focused and ran towards the counter in a hurry. Just as he turned, he spotted the last suspect cowering with his eyes covered by his hands.

"Put your hands in the air! Drop the weapon! NOW, DO IT." Wayne commanded, pulling out and pointing his taser at the man.

He complied, dropped his .357 Magnum, and put his hands up.

"House is clear." Charlie spoke into his radio.

Back upstairs, Wesley looked outside the broken window to predict where the woman escaped to.

When he looked down, he saw her.

She had been impaled on the fence.

Chapter 3

Fabian Jurewicz

Fabian had grown up to a Polish family; they had immigrated to America in the 1940s and settled in Arizona. His parents were no kind souls. His dad was abusive and his mother a criminal.

Fabian made a living during his teenage years working a part-time job at a small theatre downtown.

When he was 19, his mother was sent to prison on multiple counts of theft, shoplifting, and arson.

"We're sorry, Fabian." the police had told him.

"You're sorry? You take my mom away from me then expect me to stay with John!?" he had retaliated.

John was his father's name; he hated calling him 'Dad'.

He had spent years putting up with John's abusive behaviour. By the age of 20, enough was enough.

Fabian Jurewicz was sentenced to 4 years in prison for the murder of John Jurewicz on September 2nd, 1997.

He had stabbed him to death with a pen knife that he stole from his father's bedroom drawer the previous day.

In Prison, Fabian met a group of people his age who were in prison for similar crimes.

Released in 2000 for good behaviour, Fabian laid low and waited for his friends to be released from prison.

By 2015, all of Fabian's friends had been released, except for one; Mike Harty, who committed suicide age 23 in 2004.

One of his friends, Thomas Gazzi, thought of the idea of returning to crime. He proposed making an organization. They all agreed and made a pact to never betray the group with consequence of death.

STORM 7

Crimson

Crimson was created in January 2016. It had 4 members; Fabian Jurewicz, Thomas Gazzi, Danny Brooks and Doug Royce.

They started off with small crimes; shoplifting, pickpocketing and mugging.

In February 2016, they completed their first crime *together*. It was a cold and windy winters day and they noticed a man step out of a limousine and into the local theatre. That's when they planned what to do.

Fabian would walk up to the man and pretend to drop an item, and ask him for help. As the man helped Fabian, Danny would pretend to be another citizen who wanted to help and start talking to the man. While the man was distracted by both Fabian and Danny, Doug would swoop past and pickpocket him.

When he then notices his wallet is gone, he would immediately turn to Fabian and accuse him of stealing it. Meanwhile, Thomas would come behind the man and tell him he found his wallet, giving him his now empty wallet back. During all of this, none of the four would directly look at him. They would also wear distinct accessories to block parts of their face; an eyepatch, a scarf, or a wig with long hair.

BEN WALKER

They tested this on multiple people and it worked every time, with the person walking away and not noticing their wallet was empty until they got home.

Once they began to realize how easy it was to get away with these petty crimes, they started to step up their game.

On April 18th, 2017, Fabian Jurewicz walked into Madison Heights Hotel & Casino and gave his large suitcase to an employee to put into storage while he was waiting for his check-in time in half an hour.

Thomas Gazzi unzipped the suitcase and stepped out of it, gasping for air. He ran to the door of the room and hid in the corner.

A few minutes later, the door opened and an employee walked through with some luggage, closing the door behind him. Thomas snook up behind the employee and injected him with a tranquiliser which also caused short-term memory loss.

He quickly took his uniform and put it on, then put the employee into the suitcase and zipped it up.

Thomas left the storage room.

Half an hour later, Fabian returned to the front desk.

"I'd like to check-in, please. I already filled out the forms half an hour ago." he told the clerk.

STORM 7

"No problem, sir. Here is your room key, Room 1305. I will get a porter to bring your luggage to your room shortly."

"Thank you." he returned.

The clerk walked behind reception and noticed Thomas.

"Oh, are you new?" they asked.

"Uh, yeah. Just started yesterday."

"Okay, well can you take this suitcase up to Room 1305 for me?" he gave him the ID number of the luggage.

"Sure thing. Oh, while you're here, where can I get a new uniform? This one is a bit too small for me."

"You don't know?" the clerk suspiciously questioned.

"No uh, this was just given to me yesterday by the manager."

"Oh, well. It's the first door on the left through the staff corridor."

"Thank you!"

The clerk walked out and back towards the front desk.

Thomas took the large suitcase and loaded it onto a luggage cart.

He then started walking towards the staff only door located close to reception. That's when his phone rang.

"Hello?" he asked joyfully.

He listened for a while, then started to type in the code for the door.

"Well, thank you for your assistance. I have to carry on doing my job now, bye." he said after unlocking the door.

He hung up and put his phone back in his pocket.

Everything was going according to plan.

In the changing room, he quickly grabbed three uniforms and put two into the suitcase, zipping it back up as he put the last one on himself.

Then he continued back down the staff corridor to the freight elevator, and pressed the button to the 13th floor.

Danny Brooks walked into an unmarked room and noticed men placing money onto a trolley. They all immediately turned and looked at him. One of the men shouted.

"What the fuck are you doing in here?!"

Before Danny had time to reply, he had already pulled out his phone, and his silenced pistol.

Ding! The doors opened and Thomas casually walked down the corridor of Floor 13, glancing at each room number until he reached Room 1305.

All it took was three knocks on the door, and to no surprise the sound of a lock disengaging and the doorknob turning emanated as the door opened. Sunlight bloomed through the crack as it slowly

STORM 7

became wider. The door was now fully open, and a figure was stood in the doorway.

"Hello? Are you the porter?" he asked.

"I am, sir. Here is your luggage, right on time." Thomas responded.

"Thank you. Actually, why don't you come on in so I can get my wallet to give you a tip?"

"Oh, there's really no need sir…"

"I insist. Please, come in. Bring the suitcase."

Thomas wheeled the trolley through the narrow doorway and into the room.

"These rooms are lovely, aren't they?" the man mentioned.

"They are indeed, Mr…" Thomas left the remark open-ended.

"Crimson."

Fabian winked.

Thomas couldn't help but to smirk.

"Well, here is your tip, my man."

He produced a dollar bill with black handwriting on the corner.

"Thank you, kind sir. Enjoy your stay."

Thomas closed the door behind him, and glanced at the dollar bill.

On it was written "Deposit 22:00".

He immediately set off towards the elevator.

Fabian opened the luggage, and slightly chuckled at the sight of a half-naked man unconscious in a suitcase. However, he got on with his work.

He took the uniforms and a padlock out of the suitcase and put it in the bathroom, zipping it up and locking it. He grabbed a complimentary pen and paper from the room's desk and wrote something. After doing so, Fabian placed the note on the suitcase, put on the uniform and left.

Thomas knocked on the 'Security' door in the staff corridor.

"Come in!" a voice shouted from inside.

He walked in and saw the night guard watching the CCTV cameras while drinking coffee.

"What is it?" he groaned.

"Hi, I'm new here. Are you the Surveillance manager?"

He moaned. "Yeah, what do you want?"

Thomas slowly approached him.

"Can I just check something I saw a few moments ago? I noticed a suspicious person in the casino who might have been cheating and wanna watch the footage."

The night guard sighed. "Fine, but be quick. What time was it?"

"Around 7?"

As the night guard put his coffee down to rewind the footage, Thomas thrust his elbow into a precise spot just above his spine,

STORM 7

causing him to immediately be knocked unconscious and fall out of his chair.

While dragging the guard behind a server tower, Thomas noticed a man lurking outside the door and jumped to disable the CCTV. The sound of the door opening and closing behind him caused Thomas to immediately turn the cameras back on.

"Nice work, Tommy." Doug Royce muttered as he hung his jacket on the hanger.

Doug had applied to a job at the casino three months prior while the heist was being planned. He was the day guard; anyone who had the night shift would be the official witness if, say, a heist happened when they were on duty.

Of course, for the plan to work he'd have to also take care of the night guard at the time, so Thomas handled that.

"Is Fabian in position?" Thomas asked.

Doug switched to Camera 012; the Casino Lobby. He glanced at each corner until he noticed an employee lurking with his head down.

"That's him." he pointed.

"Excellent." Thomas packed up.

"What time did he say the deposit was?" Doug pointed out.

"Oh, here."

Thomas handed him the dollar bill, and walked towards the door. As he left, he turned inside and waved.

BEN WALKER

'Thank you for your help, Mr. Crilly!"
Mr. Crilly was the night guard.

Doug looked at the screens, and had a sip of Norman Crilly's coffee. His eyes were peeled on Camera 012.

Fabian was still leaning against the wall with his head down, until something caught his attention, and Fabian scratched his nose.

Doug knew this was the signal, and turned the camera away towards the slot machines.

Fabian noticed the camera turn, and smiled.

He heard a trolley wheeling up to him, and looked towards the source of the noise.

It was Danny Brooks, the fourth and final member. He had a silver metal trolley with a blanket over it.

Fabian looked left and right, then lifted the blanket as Danny crawled inside the second shelf of the three-tier catering trolley.

On the shelf was seven large duffel bags, and he became very uncomfortable, very quickly.

He waited for about a minute when he saw Thomas walking towards him.

They shook hands, and Thomas checked his watch.

It was 21:55.

They set off. Walking formally through the staff corridor, they reached the freight

STORM 7

elevator and pressed the lowest button. The bottom floor; underground.

The buzzing of the air conditioning running through the vents and into the elevator was an annoying occurrence and made Fabian sigh.

Ding.

The doors opened, revealing a white room with four guards in each corner, and two on either side of the gleaming, silver metallic vault door.

Fabian and Thomas wheeled the trolley down the room towards the vault, but were put to a halt by a guard with his hand out.

He checked his watch. 10 o' clock.

The guard then walked up to the trolley and lifted the bottom of the blanket to the sight of dollar bills on the third tier. If he'd have lifted the blanket any higher he would have spotted Danny lying there.

Fabian began to sweat.

After checking the trolley, the guard then pat down both Fabian and Thomas.

He turned towards his peers and nodded.

"All clear." the guard muttered.

They proceeded forward; the wheels squeaking like mice.

The two guards who were on either end both turned around towards the vault door and typed in a code simultaneously on both sides.

BEN WALKER

A sound of a tube releasing emanated from the lock system of the vault door.

The main guard who gave the group an all-clear walked up to the door, and turned the valve four times.

It opened with a thump, and as it slid away millions upon millions in cash was presented in plain view. Thomas wanted to gasp but had to remain in character.

When they finally were inside the vault, they had to take the blanket off and leave the trolley. And so, they did. As Fabian slowly lifted off the blanket the guard eyeballed him.

But the guard failed to notice Danny in time, and took a tranquiliser to the leg.

He groaned and fell to the ground, alerting the others, but they were too late. The elevator's classic ding was heard, and Doug walked out. He shot two of the guards in the back with his tranquiliser.

The remaining three guards had no clue where to look and didn't know if they were being attacked from behind or inside the vault.

Turns out it was both, as Danny and Doug both emerged and took advantage of their confusion; shooting the remaining guards.

Doug was out of breath.

"H…h…holy shit." He panted while observing the room and noticing that they were there in that moment, about to get away with thirty million dollars.

STORM 7

They all smiled, but Thomas interrupted the moment.

"Let's actually get out of here first before celebrating."

They went back into the vault and grabbed some duffel bags from the trolley, filling them with 5 million each.

"That's a lot of cash." Doug commented.

Indeed, it was.

They ran to the elevator with their bags and went back to the staff corridor on the 5th floor.

On that staff corridor was a fire exit, and they sprinted outside it and to the van.

Back in the CCTV room days upon days of footage were being deleted, and Mr. Crilly woke up confused. Upon noticing the deletion of footage, he shouted.

"NOOOO! Shit shit shit shit shit shit." He desperately tried to cancel the process.

How had this happened?

That's when the alarm for the casino set off; a staff member had noticed the employees who deposit the money into the vault tied up, with just one pinch of evidence.

A note.

"Laenge Leve Crimson".

Chapter 4

Consequences

Liam clipped off his arm sling and unwrapped the bandages. He rotated his arm like a motor. No pain.

He emanated a smile.

An applause emerged in the room. The whole squad was around him. He had a cake; it was almost like a birthday party.

After all, he had deserved it.

They were at Liam's house for a surprise party. This was the day the doctors said Liam could finally get back into gear again.

Charlie was clapping when his phone started vibrating in his pocket. Through the muttering of everyone giving small talk, he slipped away into the guest bedroom.

It was an unknown number.

"Hello?" he spoke into his phone.

No reply. Probably a wrong number. As he went to hang up, he heard something and put his phone back to his ear.

"We're watching you, Charlie Williams." a deep filtered voice returned.

"Wha...who is this?"

"We're watching you, and we know all your little secrets."

STORM 7

Charlie's pupils widened, and he started looking around.

"Prove it." he bluffed.

"It's a shame you murdered a man in cold blood without giving him chance to surrender. It's also a shame that you only arrested one person in a house of seven. The other six are now dead." the voice did not fail to provoke Charlie.

"Excuse me?" Charlie was beginning to get angry.

"Who is this? I want answers, now. Is this joke?"

"We could either expose you and your group of officers, or you could meet with us and clear your name. That way, no one would get… hurt." the voice returned. It was a small threat, but went a long way.

Charlie was beginning to sweat.

"Do you really think you can intimidate me?" he reacted.

"Oh, we know we can."

"Meet us at 4805 Hall Street in two hours, or that red dot on your chest will turn into a red hole."

Charlie slowly looked down.
The voice wasn't bluffing.

"We're so proud of you!" Liam's mother, Helen, shouted. She hugged him, but not too hastily as to hurt his shoulder.

"Thanks." Liam returned.

"Hey, has anyone seen Charlie?" Matt pointed out.

Brad tapped him on the shoulder and pointed to the guest bedroom door.

"Thanks, bud." Matt walked towards the door.

Upon opening it, he noticed that there was no one in the room.

"Are you sure he went in there?" he pointed to Brad.

Brad nodded.

"100 percent?"

Brad nodded again and raised his eyebrows to show that yes, he was sure.

"Okay." Matt trusted Brad.

He looked back into the room, and noticed that the window was open.

Odd, he thought.

"He didn't even say bye." Matt crossed his arms.

STORM 7

Chapter 5

24 Hours

Andy was in the station, biting his nails in worry.

"I told you, you have to wait 24 hours before I can fill this in." Officer James explained.

"Yeah, but he's not at his house, his wife hasn't seen him since this morning when he left for the party, and he disappeared at that party without a trace. Why hasn't he come into work?" Andy replied.

"Look, I don't know, but you have to wait another 12 hours before you can report it. I'm sorry."

Andy walked out; it didn't make any sense. How can someone just… vanish?

Charlie never came late into the office, and today of all days, you'd think he would at least stick around for the party.

"Any luck?" Wayne asked him, seeing him walk out of the precinct.

"No, and we can't declare him missing for another twelve hours."

"He'll show. Stop making a big deal out of it." Josh muttered.

"Okay, you hate him just because he's new, you do this every time we get a new team leader. Now it's time to grow up Josh." Andy growled.

Josh sighed, got in his car and started the ignition.

"Where do you think you're going?"

"Home. It's 6pm" Josh clarified.

He began to pull out of his parking spot when Commander Larson, who commandeered the LVMPD, walked outside and up to the men.

"Back inside. We need you all here." He was straight to the point.

"Why, what's up?" Wayne questioned.

"It's Crimson. We'll brief you inside."

They all went back inside and into the elevator, through the offices, and into the briefing room.

"So… what is it?" Josh was eager to get home.

"Our best detectives. They know where Crimson is going to pull off their next heist."

"When?"

"Tonight."

The squad now realized they wouldn't be going home until tomorrow.

That's when the office phone rang, which was a rare occurrence, as almost no one ever rang the Storm 7 room.

Andy got up and picked up the phone.

"Hello?" he questioned.

STORM 7

"If you think you're onto me, I'm always one step ahead." a deep filtered voice replied.

"I'm sorry?"

"Laenge Leve Crimson."

The phone hung up.

However, Andy realized that their office phone displayed the number that just called him.

They had a lead.

"Guys, get over here!" he shouted.

BEN WALKER

The Lead

Detective Harris was at her desk when Commander Larson came to her.

"We've got another lead." he said through his white moustache.

She shot up out of her chair.

"What is it?"

"We've tracked a suspicious number back to a place of interest."

"Where?!"

"Diamond Plaza."

Harris took her jacket from the back of her chair and put it on.

"What are we waiting for? Let's go!"

She walked towards the elevator.

Back in the Storm 7 office, the news had begun.

"Doug Royce, the man caught stealing a Lamborghini at last night's premiere was arrested at 9am this morning. However, interrogation has revealed that Royce had been involved in several casino heists this year, specifically the series of heists known as the Crimson Jobs."

"As a result, this has prompted a manhunt for his partners in crime. If you happen to see these people, please inform police immediately."

STORM 7

The news-anchor froze while listening to her earpiece.

"Uh, I've just been informed that we have received an anonymous video sent from Diamond Plaza on the Strip."

It played, and it was a vertically-filmed video of a hostage wearing a Diamond Plaza employee nametag. She was crying and said, "please don't hurt me".

Larson stormed into the room.

"We've got the all clear for a hot breach. You guys are going in, get ready."

Harris had heard the news on the radio in her car. Her thoughts widened; they had been wrong all along. Crimson wasn't a person… Crimson was a group.

Chapter 6

The Heist

The group was driving away for the third time in a row. Maestro Casino's money was theirs for the taking.

They had done it. Achieved the impossible.

And here they were, driving away with another vault's worth of cash.

"I'm so proud of you all! You're like a family to me!" Thomas exclaimed and laughed with high enthusiasm.

"Good work, everyone." Fabian mentioned. He was driving.

"Yeah." Doug muttered.

Crimson at this point was beyond famous. Their past heists had gained them a reputation of large magnitude.

"What's up with you?" Danny questioned Doug.

"I don't wanna do anymore heists after this. I'm done." Doug murmured.

"What?!" Thomas screeched.

"I'm done." Doug repeated, this time with more aggression.

"Stop the car." Thomas ordered Fabian. After a few seconds of contemplation, Fabian had become scared of him and pulled over.

STORM 7

Thomas unbuckled his seatbelt, opened the van door and walked to the rear. Doug gulped.

He yanked on Doug's door handle, but realized it was locked. Growling, he smashed the window.

"What the fuck, Thomas!?" Danny yelled.

He grabbed the inside handle and unlocked the door. Thomas then reached for Doug and jerked him onto the road.

"We all made a pact to never betray the group, Doug."

He pulled out a knife, but Fabian had already tackled him to the ground.

"He hasn't betrayed us!" Fabian groaned, recovering from the tackle.

"Stop!" Danny shouted. He also disembarked from the car and was sprinting towards them.

Doug took this opportunity to run. Like a cheetah running from a tiger, he ran like the wind into the distance.

Thomas was up and about to chase after him, but instead chose to not waste his time. He had a heist to get away with.

"If you tell anyone what happened here, I'll gut you like a meaty cow!" he shouted to the fading silhouette.

Fabian was panting hard. He slouched back to the car.

The rest of the journey was full of silence.

Confession

All the cash they had stolen was back at their safehouse, meaning that Doug was no longer a millionaire.

It had been a few months since he had fallen out with Crimson, and he was as paranoid as a crackhead.

After wandering around looking for ways to get out of Nevada, or even the country, Doug had finally settled on stealing a sports car and driving away for good.

Only his mind becoming delusional made it possible for him to believe such a plan would work. Poor fool.

Doug was lurking near to a film premiere, and many celebrities and their wealthy friends were in attendance. This was the perfect place. He snook behind security and ran into the parking lot near the theatre. Sprinting for his life, Doug picked the first car he saw; a 16-plate, matte black Lamborghini Gallardo.

His face lit up as he pulled out a Slim Jim and shoved it into the window. Fiddling around, waiting for the click; he heard a guard shout behind him, "Oi! Get over here, you're under arrest!".

Doug had no time to lose; he smashed the window with his elbow, sending glass everywhere. The car alarm erupted and the lights flickered inside the vehicle.

STORM 7

He yanked open the door from the inside and climbed in. But, he had no time to hotwire it. The guard was already there with a gun pointed right at Doug's head.

"You're under arrest for Grand Theft Auto. You have the right to remain silent. Anything you say can and will be used against you in a court of law. You have the right to have an attorney present during questioning. If you cannot afford an attorney, one will be appointed to you."

Doug slowly raised his arms in the air, and smiled.

He was now at the Police Station, handcuffed to a waiting room chair. While sitting there, he'd thought of a plan. He would ask to be put in witness protection if he ratted out the rest of the group. That way, he'd be clear of his crimes and be safe!

"Alright, you're up." A police officer said to him while uncuffing him from the chair and putting his other arm in as a replacement.

Doug was thrown into a classic interrogation room. Big mirror, flickering light, and metal desk.

He was cuffed to the metallic bar on the desk and given a chair.

The officer sat down opposite him.

"Anything you wanna tell us before we put you away?"

"Actually, yeah."

"You might want to… start recording."

BEN WALKER

Doug was talking for hours about the heists they did together, just like it happened yesterday. But as he proceeded through each story, a feeling of guilt flew through his body. He was ratting out his friends, who were surely going to be put to life in prison for this.

"Wow. Thank you for all this information, Mr. Royce. We will be putting you in protective custody and sending out a warrant for your buddies. You can sleep safe tonight." The officer patted Doug on his back as he walked out the room.

The door slammed shut, and Doug began to cry.

STORM 7

Last Resort

They were all gathered around watching the TV; hypnotised by it. Crimson had predicted this for months and planned a final heist. The biggest heist yet.

However, in the case Doug ratted them out they would go in loud, and out with a bang, rather than the usual stealth.

Thomas had grown obsessed with a SWAT team known as 'Storm 7'. He had stalked their leader for months and played along with their thoughts that Crimson was just one person. Unfortunately for him, those games were no longer going to be possible.

"We all know what we're going to do." Danny murmured. He was sharpening a kitchen knife.

"We're going to go out with a bang." Fabian lit up.

"It was fun while it lasted, boys." Thomas smiled.

They came in for a group hug, and went their separate ways.

Fabian dialled in a number on his phone and put it to his ear.

"Hello? It's time. Initiate the plan."

"Copy that, sir."

BEN WALKER

It was a peaceful day at Diamond Plaza. The sound of fruit machines flooded the casino lobby, and the smell of fresh carpet emanated from the hotel reception.

People were lined up waiting to check-in; it was becoming busy.

One employee, Jen, was attending to a customer when she heard the windows smash around her.

Explosions erupted from every direction. People began screaming and running in a panic.

Jen looked up and saw a man rappelling down from the skylight. He wore all black, and had thick military boots. Around his legs were armoured kneepads, and he had holsters for weapons on both sides of his trousers. On his chest was a large bulletproof vest, filled with pockets and equipment. The most notable feature of his ensemble was his midnight black balaclava and tinted ski goggles.

She was in a state of shock and could not move, but she noticed an employee run to the desk and

Suddenly, everywhere Jen looked she saw people with the same uniform rappelling. Some were running in from the main lobby door with assault rifles. Lots of shouting had occurred, and by now there were up to twenty men kicking civilians to the ground and firing warning shots into the air.

STORM 7

Jen felt an arm wrap around her throat, and a cold metallic object touch the side of her forehead. She finally screamed, escaping her trance. Choking, she attempted to break free of the grasp but realized that a gun was pointed to her head, and complied.

The force from a push launched her onto her knees, as her arms were tugged behind her back and tied together.

The man walked around in front of her and pulled out his phone.

"Please don't hurt me." Jen whispered through her tears.

The man stopped recording and put his phone away. He did not say a word.

When everyone in the lobby had been calmed down, all the men started saluting as the bell of the main lobby door rang.

Three men in a triangle formation walked inside, followed by ten guards behind them.

"Bravo!" the one at the front started clapping.

He produced a sinister grin during his joyful applause.

Jen's pupils expanded and the tears emanating from her eyes reduced in rate. This was the first time she was truly scared for her life.

The casino staff were trained for robberies, but none of this magnitude.

The joyful man from the front walked up to her and jumped on the reception desk.

He kneeled to look at her.

"Hello, little lady. What's your name? I'm Thomas." He licked his lips.

"J..J.." she was choking on her own words.

"Jen. What a lovely name." he must have read her nametag.

"Well Jen, you're famous now." Thomas spoke over the sound of a welding torch on the main door.

She had no idea what he meant until he pulled out his phone and presented a video of her, captioned with "#DiamondPlaza".

"Don't you love a good viral video?" he grinned.

Thomas got up and hopped off the desk, returning to his original position with the others.

One of the guards came up to him with a suitcase, and he opened it, pulling out a baseball bat.

Fabian became confused when Thomas handed it to him.

"What do you expect me to do with this? This wasn't part of the plan, Thomas." He whispered to him.

Thomas patted him on the back.

"I want you to beat the ever-living shit out of that woman." He replied, with a demented smile.

STORM 7

Fabian looked down at the bat, and his stomach sank.

Chapter 7

Diamond Plaza

They rushed into the armoury, putting gear on and selecting their weapons of choice. Matt grabbed an MP5 and went up the stairs.

The group met on the roof of the station. Harris was already at her car and driving down towards the Strip.

An MD 500E helicopter landed on the helipad, and they all got in. The ones who couldn't fit into the seats hooked themselves to a harness and sat on the landing skids.

The helicopter took off and straight towards the Diamond Plaza Hotel & Casino.

Clifford had to stand in because Charlie and Larson were not present.

"Okay, so we need to rappel down and onto the roof. We can work our way down the floors from there."

"Remember, we're not there to finish the job, we're there to extract the hostage. Unusually, intel suggests they've only taken one hostage, the rest are dead."

Liam was taken aback.

"Jesus Christ, they killed all their hostages?!"

STORM 7

"Unfortunately, yes. But they have left one, and we're going in to secure the building before anything else can happen."

"We need to drop Wesley and Craig off at a nearby building so they can provide sniper support.", Clifford told the pilots.

"Wayne, what's the best breaching route from the roof?"

Wayne had already studied the blueprints of the casino prior.

His best bet was to go through the door on the roof, down the stairs and through the top floor offices. Then the squad would go down two flights to reach the vault floor.

After clearing the Vault, they would take the elevator to the floor above the main lobby.

"I like it. Alright everyone, let's do this."

The helicopter landed on a neighbouring building to Diamond Plaza, and Wesley and Craig disembarked.

They setup their equipment as the chopper flew away towards the casino.

It was time.

The helicopter hovered above the Diamond Plaza Hotel & Casino, and ropes fell from it; hitting the roof.

Four ropes, eight men.

As each of the officers landed, the gravel shifted beneath their feet. Clicks and other sounds were heard as they disembarked, loaded their weapons and lined up against the fire exit on the roof.

An employee had triggered the alarm earlier, allowing the fire exit's electro-magnetic lock to automatically disengage.

Liam turned the doorknob and gently opened the door. He didn't want to alert any suspects.

Peeking into the now open building, he spotted no one.

"It's clear, but we'll need to watch out."

They all nodded.

Brad led with his ballistic shield, slowly approaching the door at the bottom of the stairs.

Liam stepped in front and used his Under-Door Camera again.

He saw up to five hostiles, all armed with balaclavas on their heads. Holding up five fingers, he stepped back and Wayne took care of the rest.

The sound of canisters sliding under the door echoed through their ears.
A few seconds of silence. Dreadfully awaiting the go ahead. He took a deep breath.

"GO GO GO".

Matt turned and lunged at the door with his foot, smashing it down with brute force.

As the door fell, the world slowed down. The sudden explosive noises flew and knocked down Matt; it was too loud. He looked around, seeing his companions rush past him to clear the room. Bright flashes originated from the barrels of their guns as they screamed something incomprehensible. There was a painful ringing in Matt's ears and it was unbearable.

The canisters activated, letting smoke fill the air and block any possibility of vision the enemy might have. The whole squad were wearing their gas masks, and thus were not affected by the impending toxicity of the tear gas. Shot after shot after shot, scream after scream. Until silence.

You could hear heavy breathing through Wayne's mask, he was worn out. They all looked around the room, pointing their barrels at each individual possible hiding spot. Bill kicked the limp arm of a body on the floor. No movement. Not even a chest inflating and deflating. "We got one down."

"Make that three." mentioned Wesley. "We got two here, I shot one."

Liam nodded at him.

"Room is clear. We have two suspects unconscious and three down." exclaimed Liam into his radio.

"Copy that. We're seeing two in the corridor. Repeat, two hostiles in the corridor." Craig replied.

"We're gonna head off coms for now, the Commander wants to speak to us." Wesley added.

BEN WALKER

Their radios went silent, and they immediately got to work. Andy went over to Matt and helped him up.

"This is a big one, lads. They know we're here now and they will do anything to get rid of us. Be smart and don't rush."

They all lined up against the doorway, signalling each other to get in position through subtle hand gestures. Wayne pulled out his flashbang and held his hand on the pin and trigger.

But before they could breach, they heard the static on Liam's radio increase.

"Hello?" Liam questioned into his radio.

All he heard in response was breathing. Heavy breathing.

"Wesley? Craig? Your radio is still on." Liam

However, it wasn't Wesley and Craig.

Someone was listening.

"Turn off your radios. All of you." He exclaimed.

"NOW."

They all did as they were told, and switched off their walkie talkies.

"Someone was listening in on us. We might… we might have a mole."

"You're bringing this up now?!" Matt shrieked.

"Yes! This operation could be jeopardized as far as we know."

STORM 7

They heard two hostiles hitting the ground through the door. Wesley had shot them with his silenced M40A1.

The noise made Andy jump, and he quietly trudged towards the door. It creaked as he opened it, peeking through the crack.

Two hostiles were dead on the floor.

"Clear.", he whispered.

They advanced through the corridor and to the stairway.

Wesley reloaded his rifle.

"That's two down.", he said to Craig.

"Corridor hostiles are down. Repeat, hostiles are down." Craig then relayed into his radio.

No response.

"Hello? Is anyone there?"

"Commander Larson, we're not getting a response from the inside team." he switched to talk to the Commander.

"Copy that. Wait five clicks then we'll investigate."

"Yes, sir."

The radio fell back to silence.

"Wait, there they are. In the corridor." Wesley pointed out, looking through his scope.

"Craig?"

He looked to his right, where Craig was staring down… at a red dot moving around on his own chest.

Wesley spotted the red dot move upwards towards Craig's head. They were both silent; in shock.

"Wesl-"

Craig's head flew backwards as a hose of blood erupted from his chin.

"CRAIG!" Wesley screamed in pain and anger, diving down to help his friend.

STORM 7

His lifeless friend.

Identity

The clunk sound created by boots stomping down the rattling stairs reverberated down the hall.

The group was running down towards the Vault floor and heard a woman crying for help through the door in front of them. Brad turned around (he was at the front of the group) and put his hand out to stop the others.

"I think they're taking a hostage towards the vault." Andy whispered.

Brad nodded in response.

"We should split up. Liam, Josh, Matt and I will keep doing down. The rest of you go clear the Vault. But be careful, they're on the lookout." Clifford stated.

"Why? Our job is to get the hostage and leave." Wayne interrupted.

"No, *our job* is to also search for any extra hostages. We can't always trust intel."

"Fine. Go. We've got this."

Brad, Andy, Wayne and Bill lined up against the door in front of them as the rest kept running down the stairs.

The wooden door had a large window that consisted of frosted glass, preventing the team from seeing through. Only the lack of any silhouettes prompted them to continue. Brad

STORM 7

slowly turned the door-handle and gently pulled back, letting the door slide open.

The now-open doorway revealed what was a TV on wheels, aimed directly at them. They looked at each other, confused.

Peering inside the room, Bill walked through the doorway.

He lifted his leg and put it down, then lifted his other leg and brought it forward; a simple walking motion. However, this caused him to touch an invisible heat sensor.

Bill heard the television in front of him turn on because of the tripwire.

The whole group stared at the TV, which now presented a person with a bag on their head, tied to a chair in a dark room.

A man walked in front of the hostage, with a bloody baseball bat. He crouched down as to match the height of the hostage, and stared directly into the camera lens.

"Hello.", he said in a high pitched, patronizing voice.

"I'm Thomas, but you can call me Uncle Tom."

He placed the baseball bat on his shoulder.

"You must be the legendary Storm 7. I've heard remarkable things about you. The way you massacred everyone in that house a few months back… that takes balls. I like that."

"I'm not here for that. You will be punished in due time. But, for now, this wonderful 'volunteer' will be punished for what you did."

He laughed demonically while pulling off the black cotton bag from the hostage's head.

The group all gasped as they realized not what was about to happen… but who it would happen to.

STORM 7

It was Charlie.

Loose Ends

Clifford led his part of the group down the stairs, and reached the floor above the main lobby.

They kicked down a door and rushed inside, peering at every corner.

"Clear." Liam said.

But it wasn't clear. They had walked right into a trap.

A net wrapped around Matt's leg and dragged him upwards to the roof, to which a bear trap was bolted onto. His foot thrusted into the trap, causing it to snap shut around his ankle, digging straight into the bone.

He screamed for his life, until his voice box almost bust.

Blood flew down onto Josh, and he began to gag.

All four men were now screaming, until Matt had been knocked unconscious from the shock.

Two guards heard the noise and ran inside. Upon spotting the men, they opened fire, hitting Josh in the shoulder and causing him to fall in agony.

Clifford and Liam ducked to cover behind a sofa.

"We're so fucked. WE'RE SO FUCKED." Liam started becoming hysterical.

STORM 7

"Get a hold of yourself! We're going to be okay."

"It's all going to be okay." Clifford repeated, but was cut off by the sound of Josh crawling towards them.

"Guys…" he grunted.

"Help me…"

Clifford's face dropped as he saw a man stand over Josh, and point his handgun at his head.

The man pulled back the slide on his Glock 22, and placed his finger around the trigger, only to be met with a bullet to the face from Liam.

He dropped to the floor; motionless.

The other guard opened fire at the leather couch with his AK47, and the bullets penetrated through it, which prompted the two to quickly run out and fire blindly at the entrance to the room.

As he was jumping out, Clifford aimed towards a silhouette he spotted through his motion blurred eyes.

Before he could fire, he fell to the ground in pain. A bullet from through the couch had hit him directly in his abdomen, penetrating through his Kevlar.

Liam opened fire on the man and spotted him falling on the floor as blood squirted across the white wallpapered walls.

He was panting, breathing for fresh air.

Turning, Liam noticed both Josh and Clifford on the floor and threw his gun down, running to help.

"Are you okay? No, this wasn't how it was supposed to happen. Please don't die on me." He cried. Tears formed in his eyes.

"Please.", he put his arm under Clifford's head.

Through his thick breathing, Clifford managed to produce some words.

"Kill… those… bastards, Liam." he choked out.

Clifford's eyes closed for the last time.

Liam sat down next to him and Josh, and sobbed.

Water mixed with blood.

STORM 7

Water Mixed with Blood

Thomas laughed maniacally.

"It's your best friend, Charlie Williams!" he yelled, overjoyed like a kid at Christmas.

Andy stepped back. He couldn't believe it.

Charlie was still in his casual wear from Liam's party, but he was covered in blood and bruises.

"But first, let's thank our sponsors for this evening!" Thomas grinned sinisterly.

On the screen flashed a picture of Wesley and Craig, laid on the gravel with bullets in both their heads.

Brad turned and threw up as the group all gasped.

Wayne screamed.

"I'll FUCKING KILL YOU!", his voice cracking through his tears.

The picture went away, to be replaced with yet another image that seemed to be taken from outside a window.

However, what mattered was inside the window, as you could see Liam hugging a body. Clifford. They also spotted a man hanging from the ceiling, and three other corpses, only one of which belonged to them.

"Another round of applause for our sponsors."

"Now, it's time for the main event!"

Thomas walked around to the back and untied Charlie. He must have wanted a fight, because Charlie immediately got up and turned to throw a punch at him. Unfortunately, he was met with a bat swing directly to his nose, and he fell onto the chair; his back cracking.

Charlie screamed in agony as Thomas walked towards the camera.

He stared directly into the lens, and whispered.

"No one was listening to your little radio except Charlie. What a shame, he was about to call for help when you went into a panic and turned your radio off."

Andy's expression turned from disgust to guilt.

"Not only that, but turning your radio off also caused Craig to be popped. I'll tell you one thing though, I was *not* expecting Wesley to off himself like that. Talk about commitment." His newly found demonic laugh turned into sinister, expressionless silence.

"It's a shame that every time you cut off a person, they die."

Thomas turned and thrust his baseball bat into Charlie, who was now on the floor.

He repeated the act, over and over, as screams of pain were heard.

All they could do was watch in horror.
Unless…

STORM 7

Brad ran towards the exit and kicked down the door, exposing the Vault room.

It was perfectly empty.

"But that's… impossible." Bill muttered from behind.

Brad was no fool. He tore down the fake image printed upon the doorframe, and immediately spotted about fifty men shoving money into bags.

Near them was a woman crying, she must have opened the vault for them.

It was her, the woman from the video.

Jen.

Brad crouched inside with his ballistic shield, putting it up to his face. All the guards turned and opened fire at him, but he was too defiant. Withstanding the force from each individual bullet, he pushed forward and heard gunshots behind him.

The team had united and a battlegrounds worth of bullets flew past his head, back and forth.

He saw bodies drop like flies in front of him. Almost every bullet fired from Storm 7 hit a hostile.

Brad started to get his hopes up, they were going to beat them.

As the blizzard of bullets darted past his head, he couldn't help but spot Jen in the middle of the crossfire, screaming for her life.

As the gunfire calmed down, a man grabbed Jen by the neck and used her as a human shield.

All his friends around him dropped dead, and he was the last one standing, with a hostage in his arms.

"Let me go, and I won't put a bullet in this bitch's head."

Andy, being the team's negotiator, put down his weapon and walked slowly towards the man.

"See, I'm unarmed. Drop the weapon."

"Tell your friends to leave. Now." The man demanded.

"Fine."

Andy turned towards the guys, who were all pointing their guns at the man's face. He nodded, and they put them down and walked out, keeping a very close eye on the hostage-taker.

Brad backed out.

"Look, this doesn't have to be this way. We'll let you go if you put down the weapon."

The man took off his balaclava.

He had blonde hair, a stubble and an expression that showed instability. Not good.

"Please." Andy reached out for the weapon.

He lowered his grip on the gun, eventually dropping it into Andy's hands.

"Very good. Very… good. Thank you." Andy stopped sweating.

STORM 7

The man let go of Jen, and she ran for her life outside the room.

It was just Andy and him. As anyone would do, Andy immediately punched the man around the face and subsided him onto his knees, placing handcuffs on both his wrists.

He walked outside the room to find the rest of the group handcuffing Jen and leaving her there.

"Stay here, it's for your own safety, Madam." Wayne insisted.

Bill was staring outside the window and at the view of the city.

Brad came up to him and gave him a hug.

By now, both Wayne and Andy had joined in for a group hug. They all began crying.

"It's gonna be okay." Wayne broke through his tears.

"They're in a better place."

"Come on, we need to finish this." Bill sniffled.

They walked down the stairs, to the main lobby.

Instead of his tapped radio, Andy opted to call the Commander on his phone.

It rang.

"Commander, it's Andy, me and three others are all that's left, Liam is unaccounted for."

Silence.

"I'm sorry, Andy." Larson responded, very clearly taken back by the news.

"We've got the hostages, but we need something."

"What is it you need?"

"A distraction in the main lobby, pronto."

"Got it."

Larson was heard shouting to the military.

"Alright, men! We're going in! Storm 7 have secured the hostage."

They placed explosive charges on the main door and stood back.

It was time.

STORM 7

Brad, Andy, Bill and Wayne ran down the stairs and barged into the door, blasting it open.

They were finally in the main lobby, and spotted a man in the middle sat on the floor, surrounded by at least a hundred guards. Laid next to him were two corpses.

The man looked up towards them and laughed.

It was him. It was Thomas Gazzi, the psychopathic killer who took over Crimson and turned it into a cult.

The corpses beside him…

Fabian Jurewicz and Danny Brooks.

His partners-in-crime, dead on a red carpet. Thomas had truly grown delusional.

"Hello, boys." he flamboyantly called up to them.

"How do you expect to win?" Andy shouted down.

"All this murder, all this killing and slaughter of innocent people, for what?"

Thomas seemed shocked by such a silly question.

"Why, power of course!" he patronized them.

"I'm going to quote an idol of mine." Thomas returned.

"'There is no inherent right or wrong in this world, those labels are just artificial constructs. Right and wrong are held by positions of authority. That is the way it's always been.'"

"Doctor Franken Stein spoke like a buffoon, but he had a point."

"Why stop the chaos if you're going to be engulfed into it one way or another?"

"I'm not going to be on the receiving end of a polluted world's mess. Might as well ride it out, like a wave dragging a little boy's corpse away from the shore."

"You're sick, Thomas. Not the world. You. You need professional help." Andy stated.

"I'm only sick of you telling me what I am." He growled.

"I've had enough of this. Men, kill them."

The guards all pointed their assault rifles up towards the railing the group were watching them from.

"We're not going down without a fight." Wayne smiled.

The lobby doors exploded off their hinges, and smoke and stun grenades detonated, sending the entire room into a frenzy. No one could see; all were deafened by the amount of gunfire heard from the panicking guards.

As the smoke died down, the group saw masses upon masses of corpses. Everyone in the room was dead, except for one. Thomas was missing; he had escaped.

STORM 7

Epilogue

Thomas Gazzi ran through the casino towards an escape hatch. Crimson had hired builders to dig underground the casino and create an underground network for escape.

Turning the corner around a stack of fruit machines, he looked hastily for the hatch.

Only to be greeted by a man covered in bruises. His lip was bust, and his clothes dampened in blood.

It was Charlie Williams, the man he had stalked for months.

Charlie cracked his knuckles.

"Hello, Thomas. Or was it Uncle Tom? I forget, you knocked the memory right out of me.", he smirked. He had been waiting for this.

He grabbed Thomas by the neck and forced a powerful connection between his knee and Thomas' nose.

A crack was heard, as blood ran from his nose.

"Oh no, did I break something? So sorry.", Charlie drained Thomas of energy with a fast punch around the face. He felt his skull and the skin bouncing into it.

Thomas toppled to the ground, teeth and blood flying out of his mouth.

It was over.

Charlie walked into the main lobby with Thomas unconscious over his shoulder.

The group gasped and ran down to hug him, as he carelessly dropped Thomas onto the floor, who landed with a thud.

A hug was all he cared about.

STORM 7

MORE FROM THIS AUTHOR

BEN WALKER
THE FALLEN ONES

Jack Rotner is a normal teen from Manchester, with a normal family, and normal friends.
The only notable difference; he's dead.

MORE FROM THIS AUTHOR

BEN WALKER
THE FALL AND THE IMPACT

The Fall and the Impact is a historically fictional short story told from the perspective of a bomb in World War II.

BEN WALKER

Thank you for reading this novella. I'm grateful that you took some time out of your day to read something I put together in just over 2 months. 400 hours of my life dedicated to this one little word document on my computer. 400 hours is double my playtime on Rainbow Six Siege, but it does include writers block time so you never know.

However, this has been, by far, some of the most fun I've had working on something since forever.

Thanks to all credited on my Special Thanks page, and a huge thanks to yourself for reading.

I hope you enjoyed this little story I created in my bedroom one day and fabricated into a novella.

- Ben Walker

Printed in Great Britain
by Amazon